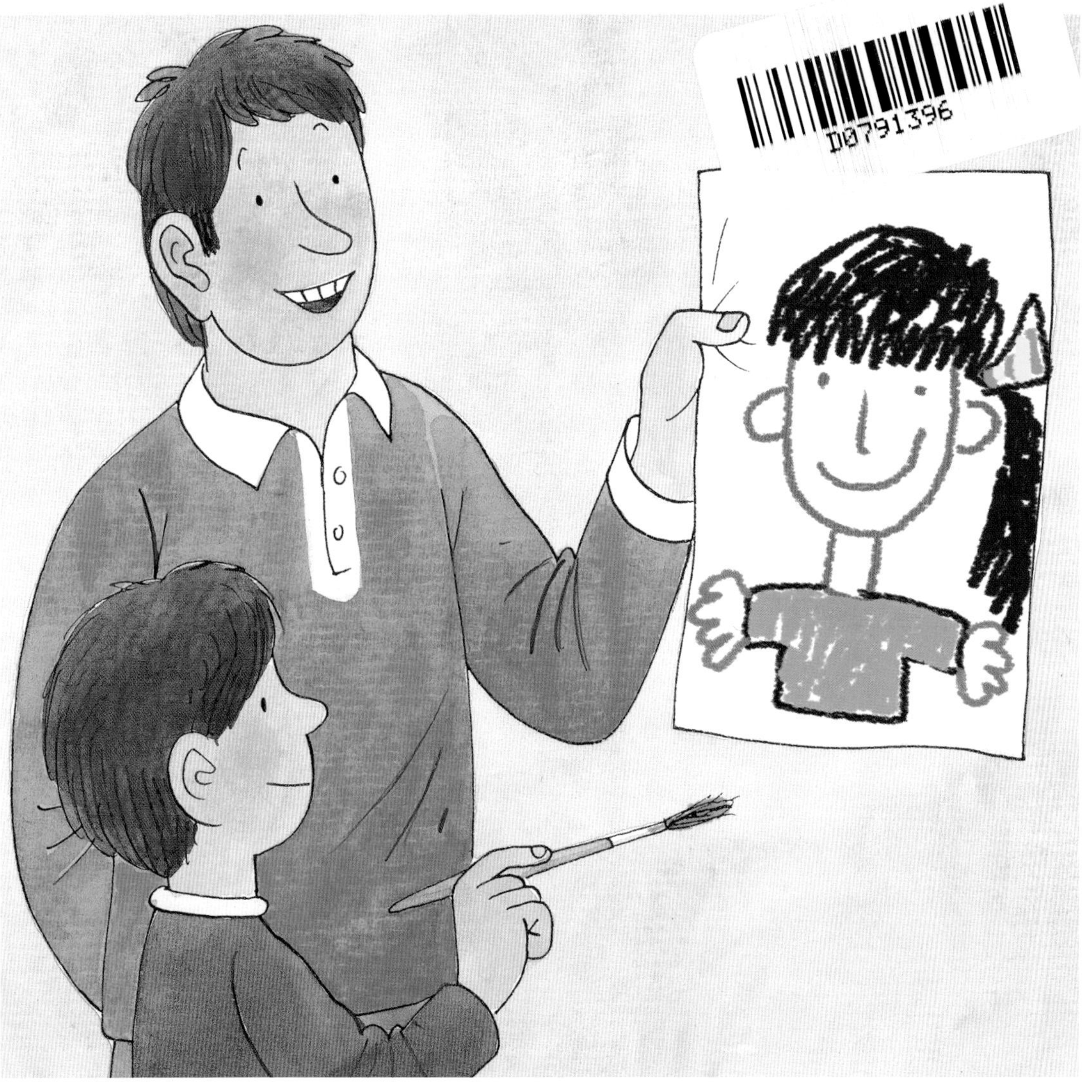

Chip did this.

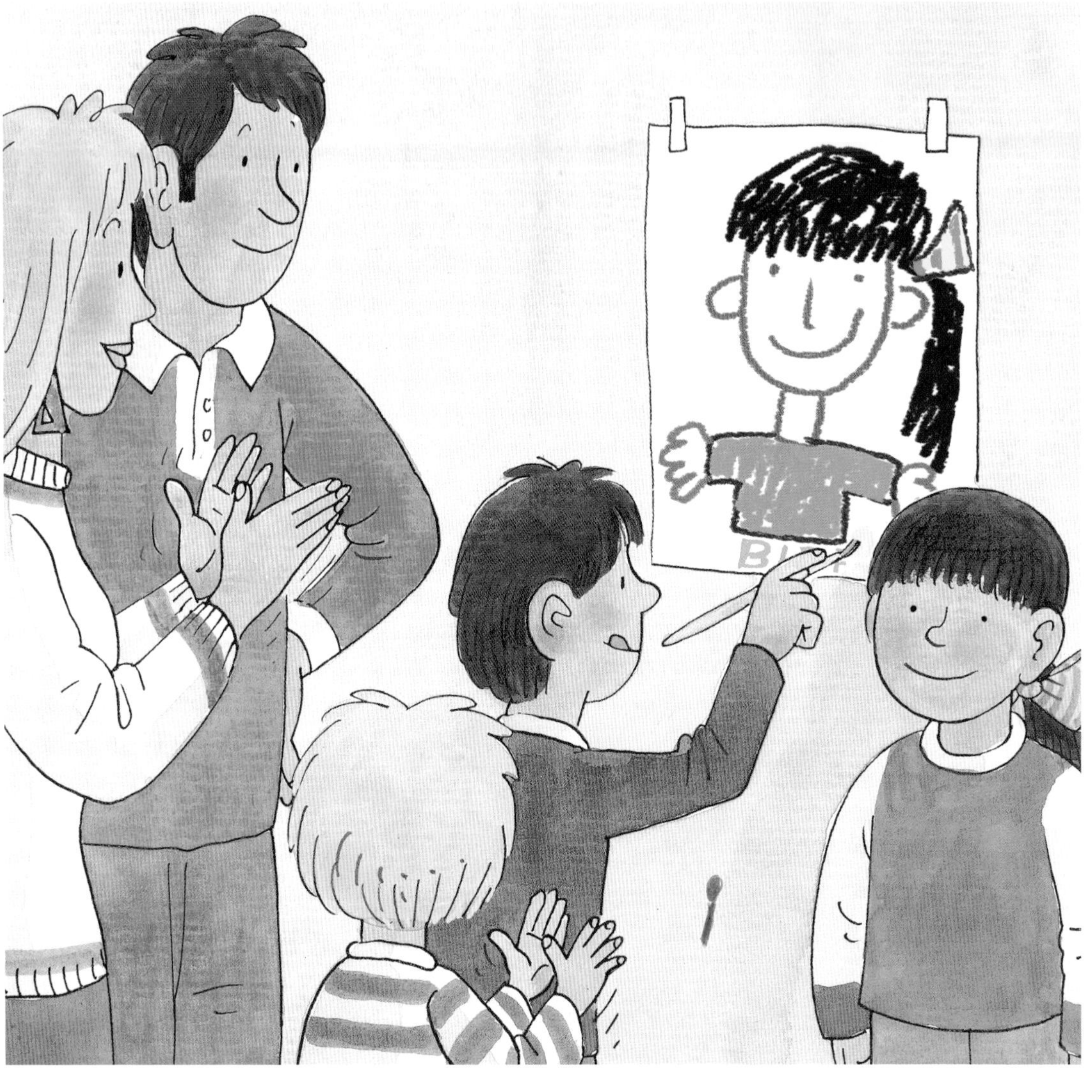

It is Biff.

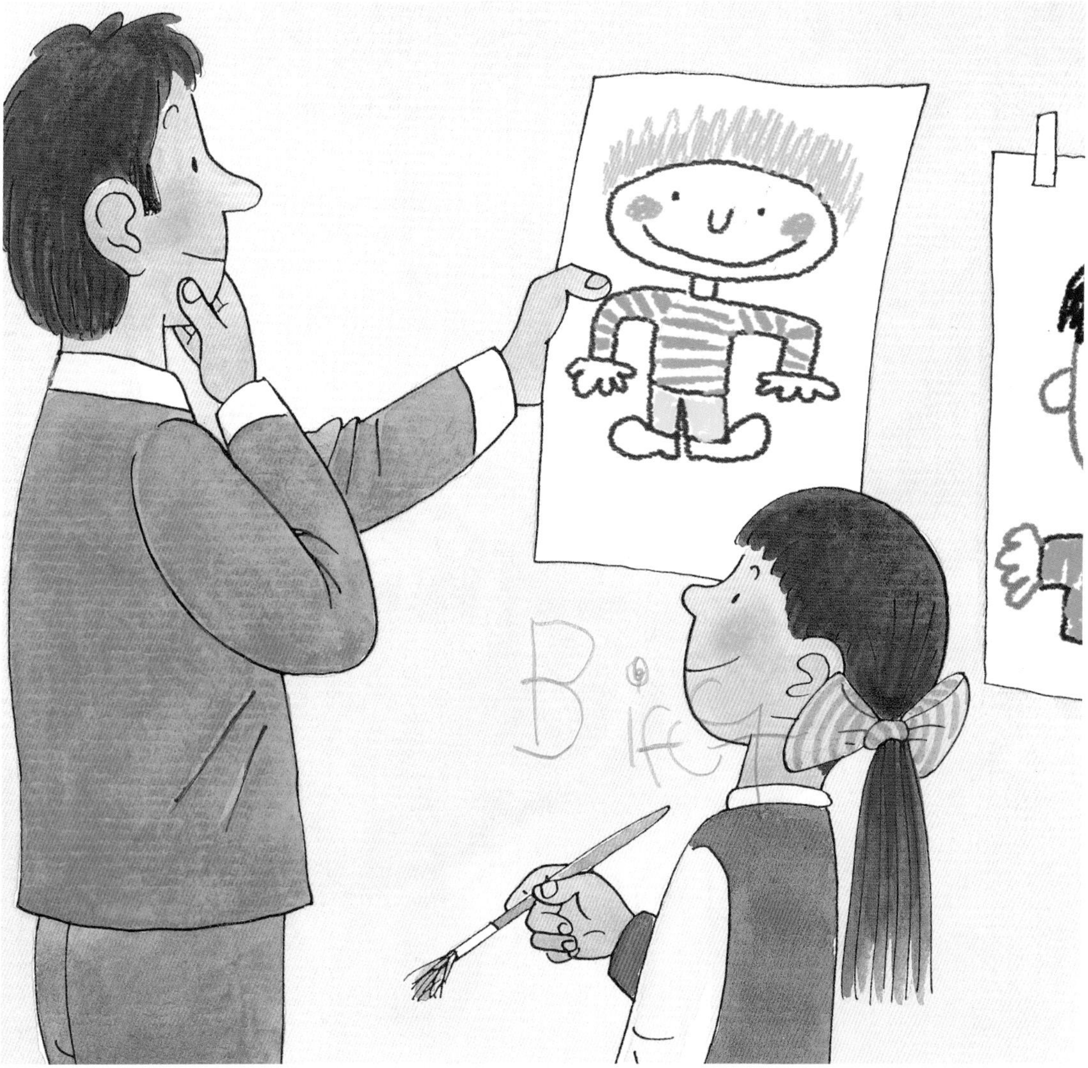

Biff did this.

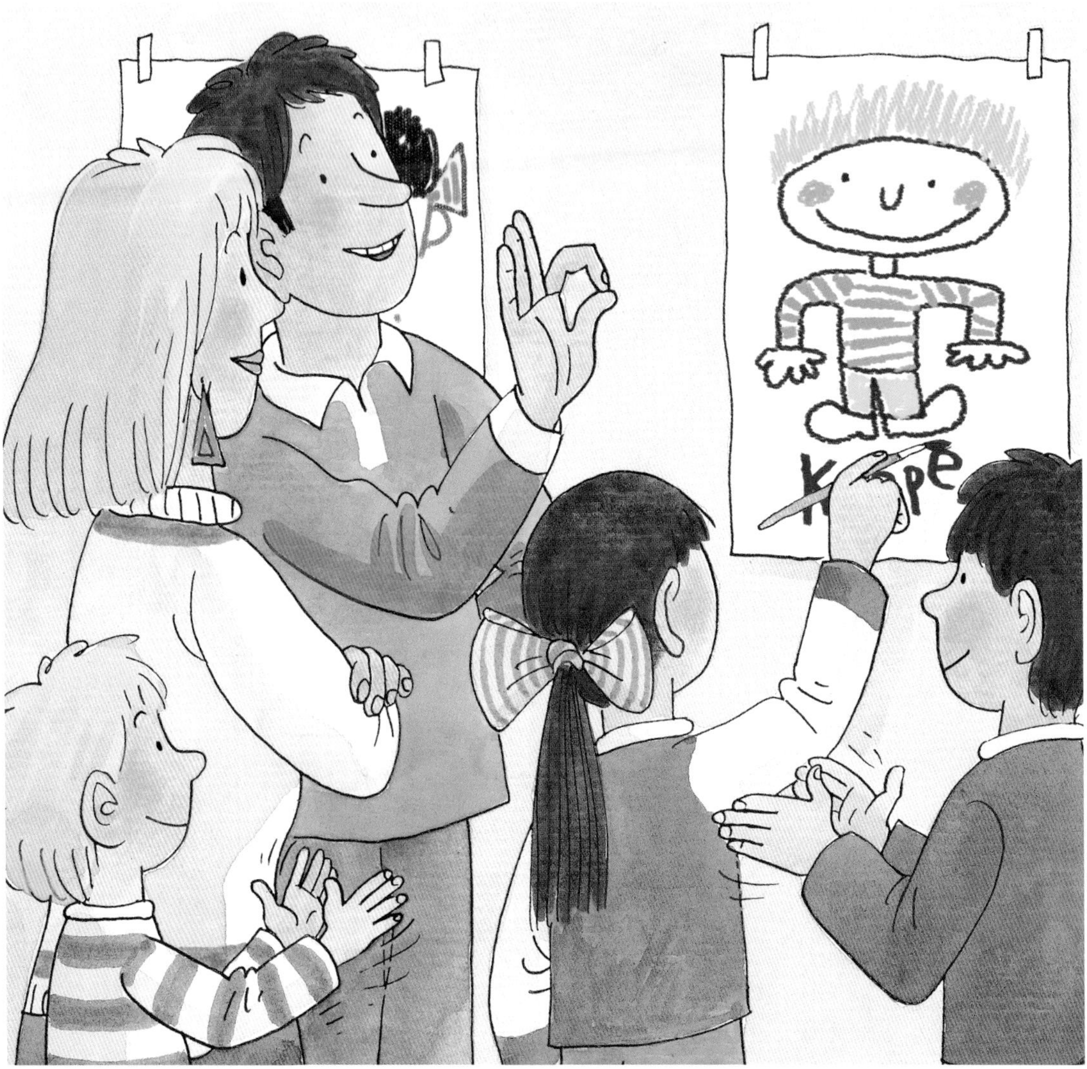

It is Kipper.

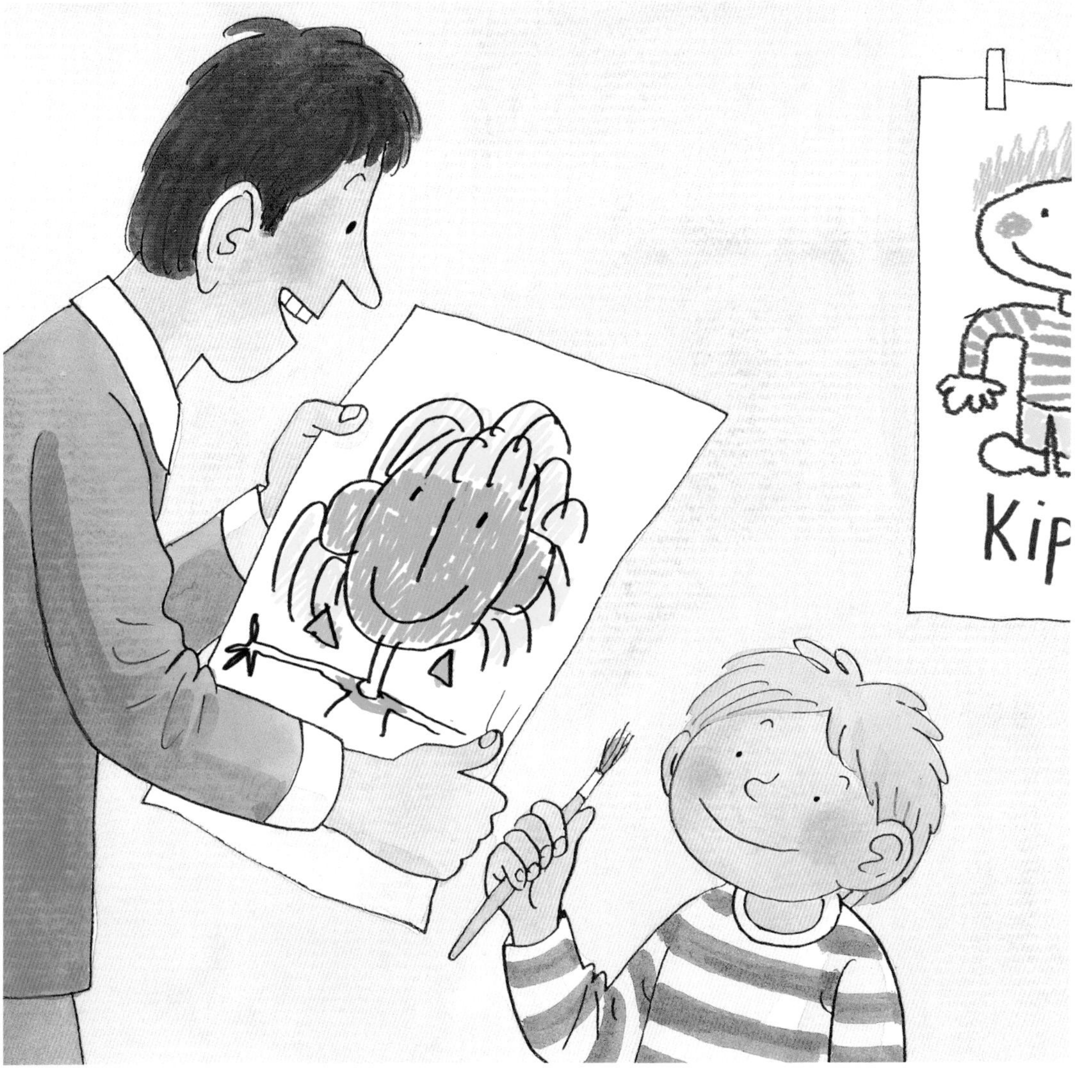

Kipper did this.

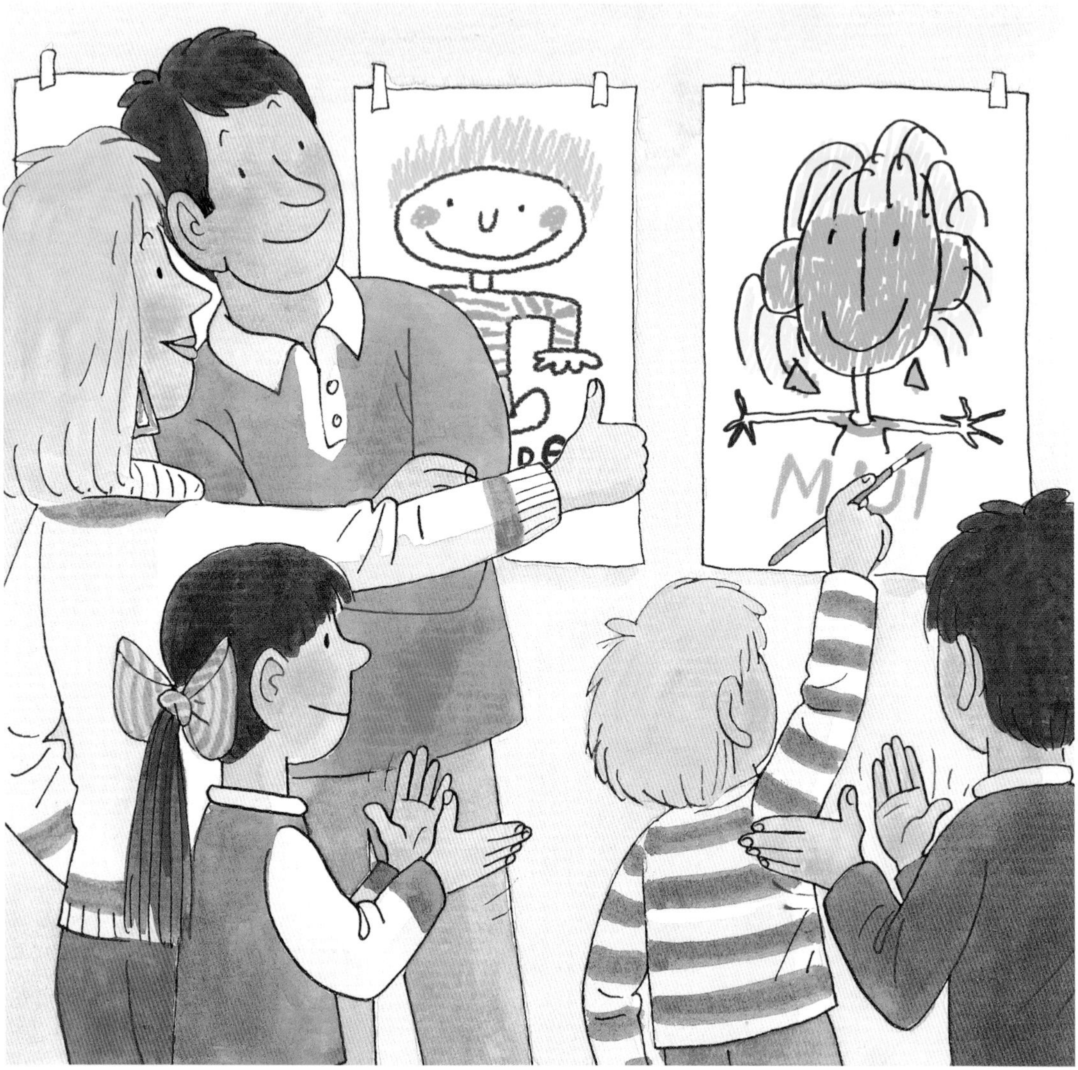

It is Mum.

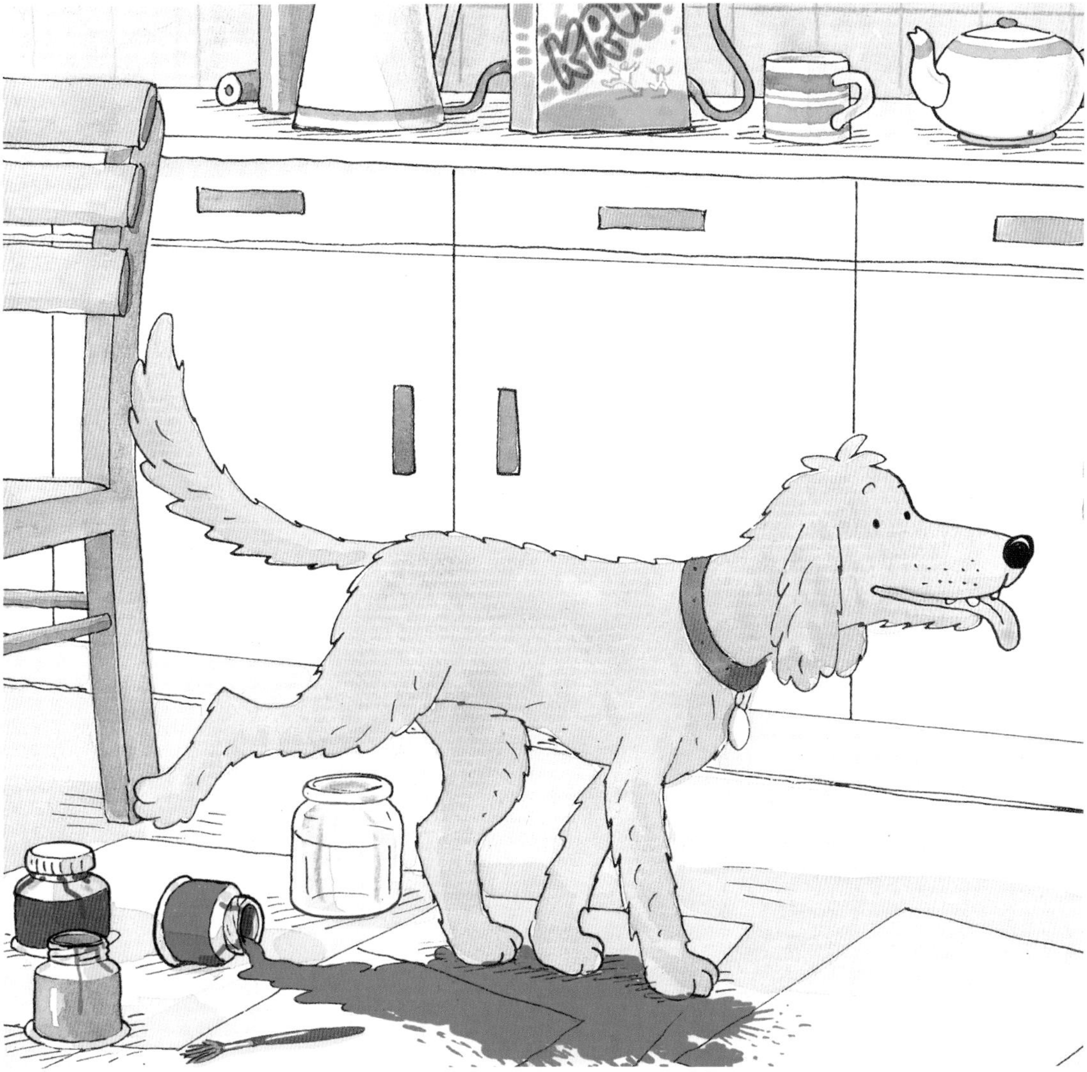

Oh, no!

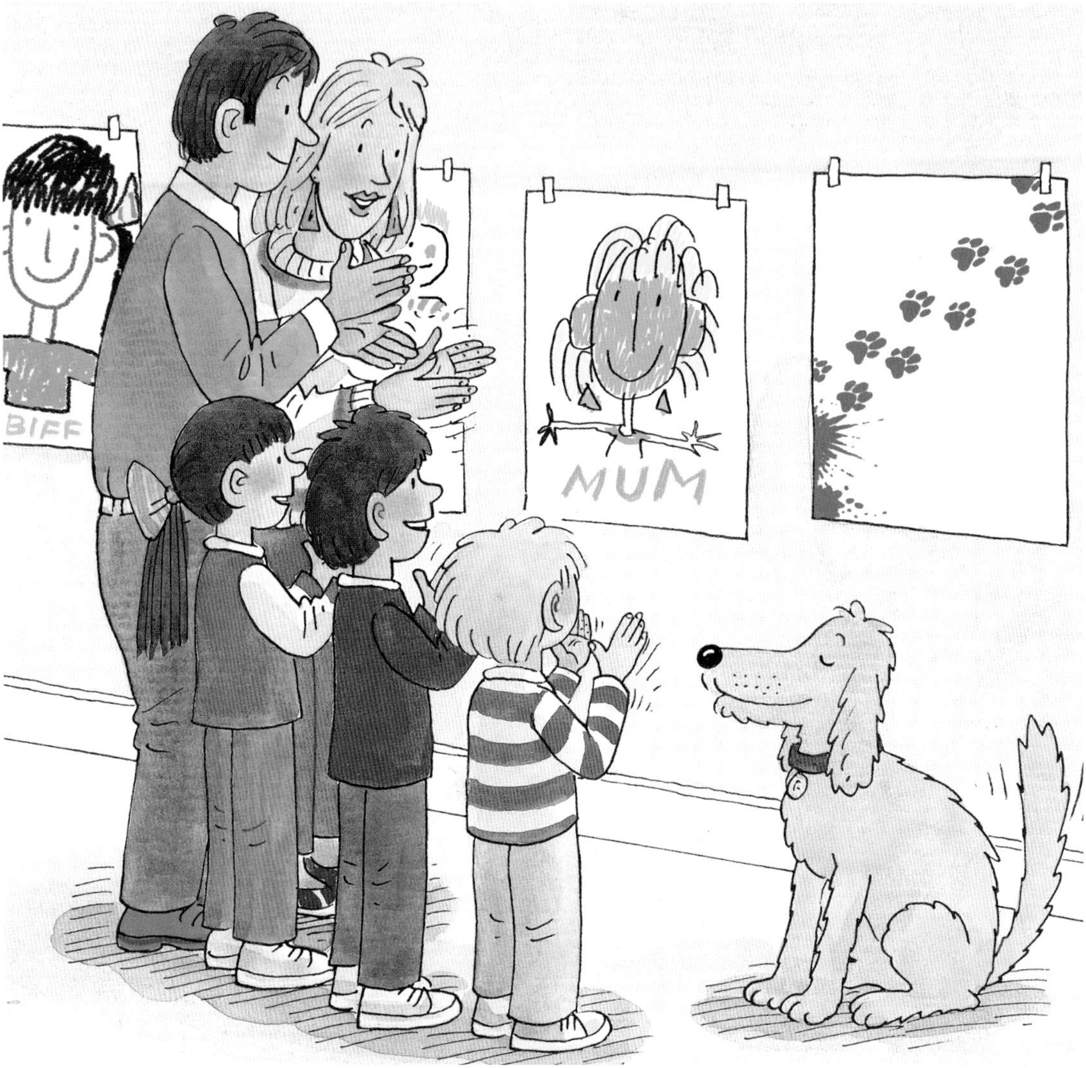

Floppy did this.